# 12 Hours

A Short Story

Lee DuCote

# 12 Hours

Raccoon Bend Publishing Benton Louisiana

ISBN-13: 978-1-7377911-2-6
Editor: Jennifer Jacks

In Publication Data: DuCote, Lee

FICTION / Short Story / 20th Century Printed in the United States.

# Chapter One

In the towering shadows of a Live Oak, stood an elderly man. He fanned his shirt back and forth against his body, trying to cool down from the brutal heat that the south was so famous for in August. With an old weathered wooden cane in one hand and a 1960s medium size suitcase in the other, JC watched cars speed by on Fairview Avenue, wondering why people were always in a hurry. Fairview was a street that never lost its reputation for housing some of the area's wealthiest people, a road coveted by many moving to the second largest city in Louisiana.

JC Davis was a former cobbler from St. Louis, Missouri, a man passionate for seeing things through. He had looked forward to this trip since making reservations three weeks ago, a trip he was also deeply concerned about.

"Mr. Davis?" A younger thin man walked out onto the lawn across the street from JC.

"That would be me," JC replied, carefully stepping off the curb and toward the two-story white house with crimson trim. "I don't remember it being white." He pointed at the house with his cane.

"It was painted white years ago, I believe before it became a bed and breakfast."

JC stopped in the middle of the street. "It looks nice. But I'll be truthful, I liked it brown."

"Yes, sir, I am sure you have great memoirs of the place back then." The man reached out to take JC's suitcase. "Be careful here. It's a slick spot with all that loose gravel." He nodded to where the driveway met the blacktop.

JC laughed. "Yep, busted my butt right here sixty years ago." Then, he stuck out his old, leathered hand. "JC Davis."

"Pleasure to meet you, Mr. Davis. My name is Gary Smith."

"Oh, you're the young man I spoke with on the phone. You own the place now."

"I don't know about young," Gary answered, laughing. "But we have the room you requested. If you like, the third story room is also available, and we can . . ."

JC interrupted him. "No, no. Thank you, but the room I reserved is perfect."

They strolled up the drive to the front door, where Gary held it open for JC who motioned him to go in first. JC turned back, glancing at the street, and with a memory flash, the busy street turned from sleek new cars and flashy trucks to street cars, Buick sedans, and 78 Fords. The white wall tires and the roar of a solid V8 brought a grin to the old man's face. He stood for a few minutes reminiscing the past until the heat reminded him it was 1999.

"I'm sure there have been many changes since you last stayed here." Gary set JC's suitcase at the foot of the stairs and nodded toward the parlor.

JC wanted to answer, but his voice left him with his breath. Seeing through the many changes on the inside, he could visualize it like it was sixty years ago. The old smell, the feel of the wooden banister, and the creaking floor below the stairs rattled loose an emotion he hadn't felt for nearly eleven months.

"A couple from Arkansas and a businessman from Texas are joining us tonight. You're the first one here. Can I get you something to drink?" Gary asked.

"Ice water is fine." JC walked into the parlor admiring the baby grand piano tucked into the corner of the room adjacent to the fireplace.

"The town has many great restaurants. If you tell me what you're hungry for, I can recommend something," Gary shouted from the kitchen.

"Is the Meat and Three still open?"

"Yes, sir. It was moved years ago with the interstate going in, but the good news is that it's just six blocks north of here."

JC smiled remembering that it was only seven blocks away, seven blocks he had made just once. Gary continued to provide him with information he already knew as they made their way to the stairs. The main dining room had changed from old wooden floors and high ceilings to carpeted floors and décor hanging from a chandelier that hid the height of the ceiling.

In the middle of their conversation, a ringing came from the front door, and just like that, JC went from the center of Gary's attention to standing in the room alone. Being alone was ok with JC as he had made the reservation for some private time. By the sound of the welcoming from Gary, JC figured it was the couple that he had mentioned earlier in their conversation.

The talk turned quiet, and the footsteps on the stairs assured him that he would be alone for a moment more, and with that, he slipped into the kitchen, a place guests weren't allowed the last time he was there. The wallpaper had been recently added, but the appliances had not been touched since the late 70s. The layout hadn't changed and neither had the memories.

"I believe our couple might have had too many hours of traveling," Gary said, joining JC.

"I'm sorry. I was just looking around."

"You are welcome anywhere in the house; don't be sorry."

JC grinned a thank you, then, "Too many hours?"

"A tad bit on edge. Perhaps a pre-dinner cocktail will help them."

"Maybe I should get unpacked." JC hinted he was ready to see his room. Gary motioned for him to follow, and together they climbed the stairs that creaked with every step.

The upstairs was quant and homey, with the only door shut that of the young couple. Gary stepped in the doorway of JC's room and allowed him to go first. He entered the room looking around like an elementary child would in a museum, taking slow steps and scanning the room with his mouth open.

It had been sixty years, three months, fourteen days, and roughly ten hours since JC closed the door, leaving the room and starting a life that would top most kings in the world. Gary took notice of his overwhelming reaction and quietly excused himself leaving JC alone with his moment. He placed the old light blue suitcase on the bed, fought with the latch to open it, and removed an eight-by-ten black and white portrait of a beautiful brunette from the late 1930s. The picture was framed with dark mahogany wood with a faded mat outlining the picture.

"Well, Mae, here's to finding you." He touched the face of the young girl and then placed the framed picture on the night table with tears whelping up in his tired green eyes.

# Chapter 2

A loud voice from downstairs startled JC from an evening nap; he fought to untangle the white-laced blanket he had covered himself. The window unit buzzed with a strain to continue pushing cold air into the one bedroom, and with shaky hands, JC managed to turn off the ac unit. The voice from downstairs had a strong bass that managed to penetrate the walls of the bed and breakfast and stir him from his rest. JC knew by the loud outburst of laughs it must be the salesman from Texas.

After a few deep breaths, he left his bedroom slowly and quietly, pulling the door shut. His soundless retreat wouldn't have mattered, not with the over-loud conversation that echoed from the parlor just below the stairs and to the right. Cradling the banister with his left hand, JC took each step at a slow pace, not because he was careful, not because he was buying time to meet the Texan, but to reminisce the countless times he descended the twenty-seven steps.

"You must be the fellow from St. Louis!" The Texan's voice grew louder, when pronouncing Louis.

"I am," JC answered, not yet to the bottom of the stairs.

"Come on down here and visit with these youngsters and myself. Word has it you stayed here sixty-something years ago," he announced to the entire house. "Boy howdy, I was just a young runt sixty years ago. Probably chasing rabbits and eatin' bugs." He turned to the young girl who was pushed back into the couch, trying not to be recognized. "You ever eaten a grasshopper? Juicy creatures, but they have a hint of cocoa beans."

"Alright, Mr. Jones, I doubt these folks want to hear about eating insects. How about a pre-dinner cocktail?" Gary asked the young couple and JC.

"You need to try one of them beers from a local brewery, made right here in town. They call them breweries or microbreweries. You see, they buy their hops from out there on the west coast. . ."

"So, I take it you want your usual?" Gary interrupted Mr. Jones.

"You bet!" He looked back at the couple and JC. "I stay here a lot. Old Gary knows what I like and seems to put up with me."

"I'll take a beer," the young man said.

"Water, please," the young girl answered in a soft mousy voice.

"Anything red would be nice," JC said.

"And not Kool-Aid! Right!" Mr. Jones replied, then burst out laughing at his own joke. Gary smiled at JC, assuring him that he understood he would like a glass of wine. "By golly, I have lost my manners. My name is Butch Jones." He held out his big hand to the elderly man who was just starting to sit.

"JC."

The young man sat up. "My name is Troy." Then, after an awkward moment, the young girl elbowed him in his side. "What?"

"You're supposed to introduce me too."

"Oh, and this is Rebecca."

"We're going to call you Becky for short." Butch bolted out and then looked around to the kitchen. "I better make sure Ol' Gary is putting our beers in frozen mugs." He left the room giving a lecture on why frozen mugs were so essential and how they came about years ago. JC laughed, not knowing if his history was correct.

They sat without a word for what seemed like an hour before Rebecca broke the silence. "What brings you back to this house?"

"Don't ask someone their business. He might not want to say," Troy scolded.

Rebecca started to sink back in the couch, but JC spoke up. "Please ask. That's part of staying in a bed and breakfast. You get to learn other people's stories."

"And because it's cheaper than a hotel," Troy volunteered.

"Maybe." He looked at Rebecca, who continuously flipped a strand of blonde hair that kept falling in her face. "I am searching for an old friend." He paused. "My wife passed a few months ago."

Rebecca just nodded with his answer, and to JC's surprise, Troy spoke back up, "I'm sorry to hear about your loss. . . were you married long?" Rebecca smiled at her young husband's change of heart about questions.

"Fifty-one years."

Troy looked down while fumbling with a napkin he was holding. "Wow, that's pretty cool."

"Yes, I believe it's pretty cool too." JC smiled, then changed the subject. "What brings you two here?"

They stared at each other, then Troy spoke, "We have some business here."

Obviously, they didn't want to talk about their visit, so JC changed the subject. "Where are you from?" He gave them a quick escape from the previous question.

"I wonder what kind of beer they have?" Troy stood, avoiding even that question, and left the room.

JC and Rebecca glanced at each other for an awkward moment before JC broke the moment by moving toward the small baby grand piano and running his hand over the clear lacquer finish. His memory left the room for a moment, thinking back to when he first visited here and the young lady who softly played the ivory keys. It was one of his favorite instruments, and ever since his grandson introduced him to the Pandora station classical piano, he has listened daily.

"Do you play?" the mousey voice asked him.

"No, but I know someone who once did."

He heard the couch shifting as Rebecca climbed up and made her way to the bench behind the piano. "What would you like to hear?"

A warm gratitude of emotion swift over his chest. "I'd be honored if you knew any Bing Crosby? Especially Have I Told You Lately That I Love You."

The young girl smiled and began playing the 1930s hit like she had played it every day since birth. JC's eyes widened in amazement that she knew it so well, more so as she hummed the lyrics along with her playing. Joining in, he tapped his fingers on the piano and hummed with her, and within the second chorus, they slowly began singing the words.

Butch appeared from the kitchen quicker than a child could enter a living room on Christmas morning. He was a Texan born and raised, but obviously the sounds of a piano pulled him out of his country demeanor, because within seconds his loud voice overpowered the old man and the young girl. But he knew the song word for word, and that made JC happy, since he had sung the song in the living room many years ago.

# Chapter 3

Gary announced to the group that supper was served, and they made their way to the table. JC and Butch stood while Rebecca made her way to the mahogany table; Troy sat first but quickly stood back up after Butch cleared his throat. Once everyone was seated, Gary backed out the kitchen door, a tray of salads in his hands. He gracefully set a salad in front of everyone, then presented each person with fresh cracked pepper.

"Ol Gary is one of the best cooks around. That's why I keep coming back," Butch said to everyone while motioning for Gary to continue adding pepper to his salad.

"Other than coming here, why do you keep coming back to this area?" Rebecca asked.

"Don't ask people their business," Troy replied.

Butch sat up in his chair. "No, no. You have to ask if you want to know. That's the great part of staying at a B and B." He smiled. "I'm a salesman. Been selling oilfield parts for nearly thirty years now. My dad sold parts, and my granddad was part of the oil boom in Texas. Yes, sir, granddad lived in Beaumont, Texas, around 1920, and well, that's where oil started pumping through our veins." Butch took a big swig of his beer. "So that's why I keep coming back to this area. Lots of oil around these parts, and not many salesmen either. Why I practically have the whole area to myself. Some years I make big money, and I mean big money. Other years I barely make enough to drive over here from home."

"Where is home?" Rebecca asked in a mousy tone.

"Kilgore, Texas! I got married early in life." He paused and pointed to the young couple. "My advice to any young couple, get married early and get married broke! That way, money isn't the drive of the marriage."

"That's great advice," Gary replied, setting down everyone's meal in front of them.

"Yep, got married to my Misses dead broke, and we had four kids. Three of them are married, and one, well, I'm not sure what she's doing. Lives up in Tulsa with her friend. All of them are happy, and the youngest is following in my footsteps. Won't be long he'll be staying here with Ol Gary." He took another swig of beer and started cutting his steak. "What about you, Becky? What brings y'all here?"

"We are . . ." She started and then was cut off by Troy.

"We are just passing through," he said, creating an awkward silence.

"JC looks like your turn. You are the mystery man; what brings you back?" Butch asked.

Wiping his mouth with his napkin, "Oh goodness. You people might think I'm a horrible person."

"I doubt that," Rebecca answered.

"Well, first, I married my late wife over fifty years ago and had a great marriage. Raised three great kids and traveled when we could—great times. A few years before I met my late wife, I had met a girl who I thought was the one.

But things didn't work out, and it steered me to my dear, beloved wife."

"We gotta have more than that! Did your late wife know about this girl?" Butch asked.

JC laughed at Butch's instant enthusiasm. "I'll make a long story short. On my wife's death bed, she instructed me to not live alone and find someone to spend the rest of my life with. So, seven months after her death, I decided to come here to find the girl I thought was the one and see where she is in life."

"Your wife dies, and you come here to find a girl you thought you loved sixty years ago?" Troy asked in a disapproving tone.

Rebecca gave Troy a dirty look, then turned to JC. "I sense a love story; go on."

"It is. Mae was her name, and she worked here when this place was a boarding house. I had stopped here on my way to bootcamp. I remember walking in the door and setting my rut bag beside that baby-grand piano." He pointed to the piano. "She walked out of the kitchen with drinks for another visiting couple. Our eyes locked, then she gave me a smile that was permanently etched in my mind. She had long flowing brown hair that paired with her green eyes; she was the prettiest thing I had ever seen. I was only here for twelve hours before shipping out, so naturally, it wouldn't have given us any time to visit. But the other couple kept to themselves, leaving me time to talk to that beauty."

Gary returned with dessert, and JC continued after everyone tried a bite. "We ate together that evening, and when we finished, I asked her to take a walk with me. I was a very inquisitive young man back then, so I asked her a million questions about herself. And being a good sport, she answered all of them."

"That's not being a good sport; she was crushing on you." Rebecca smiled, engrossed in the story.

Laughing, "Well, I wasn't very good at figuring things out like that. But looking back, I would agree. We stayed up all night talking and sneaking sweets from the kitchen. She said she felt like she had known me forever, and I felt the same. The following day I was scheduled to leave after breakfast, so she walked me to the bus stop once she was done with her duties. She gave me this note she had written earlier that morning." He pulled an old yellow piece of paper from his pocket. The ink was faded but still readable. He read it out loud. "'JC, you are the kind of guy I would like to get to know better. Please write.' And she included her address. Back then, you didn't have much time to write in bootcamp, but I wrote as much as possible. She wrote back for the following few weeks, but we lost touch when I was moved for additional training. I figured she had decided that I was just an idea. Then four months later, and after several letters from me, she wrote."

He pulled another letter from his pocket. "'JC, I hope this finds you. I am sorry I haven't written sooner. Honestly, I wasn't sure if I should write you at all. I am afraid I haven't been honest with you. After such a great time together, I didn't want to ruin our friendship with this. I am pregnant. My parents sent me here to go through my pregnancy, have my baby, and put him or her up for adoption. I didn't tell you because I found myself attracted to you in a short time. I understand if you don't write back, but I will always answer if you do. Mae'." JC folded the note and put it back in his pocket.

"Wow! What did you do?" Rebecca sat closer to the edge of her seat.

JC shrugged his shoulders. "I wrote her, and she wrote me. Through her pregnancy and through birth. She had a boy. But . . . she broke it off. She decided to keep the baby and told me I should be with someone who didn't have a kid. I wrote several more times, but she never responded, and eventually, the letters returned, unopened. So, I moved on and met my bride after I left the service and went on with life."

"This is crazy, you are here to find someone that you haven't spoken to in sixty years?" Troy asked.

"Yep."

Butch stood up. "And we are going to find this Mae. I'm in!" He exclaimed.

"You're in?" JC asked.

"Yes, sir, my customers can wait. We got a girl to find!" Butch answered, pulling a cigar out of his shirt pocket.

"Me too," Rebecca replied.

"I don't want to take your time. I'm not sure where she is in life or if she is still alive." JC gave a sad smile.

"Well, we are going to find out!" Butch started to light his cigar, but Gary ran him out the door first.

# Chapter 4

The following morning JC went through his morning rituals and picked out a shirt he'd had dry cleaned before his trip. To his surprise, everyone was already at the table eating breakfast; Butch held up his coffee cup, insinuating good morning. There was a spot reserved for JC next to Rebecca, who didn't share the smiles with Butch.

Butch swallowed his mouth full of bacon. "You ready to find Mae this morning? I hope you have been practicing what you are going to say." He paused. "Hey, what if she's married?"

"Honestly, I am expecting it. I'll just say hello and move on. But I'll never know unless I find her," JC said. Then, turning to Rebecca, "How are you this morning?"

She looked at him with puppy dog eyes. "Troy doesn't want to go. We have an appointment this afternoon." She looked down at her plate.

"Come with us this morning, and we'll have you back. What's your appointment?" Butch asked.

Troy piped up, "She and I have something this morning also. And we'd like to keep our business to ourselves."

Butch held up both hands. "Hey, your business is your business. Didn't mean anything by it."

The awkwardness settled everyone into eating breakfast and sharing the morning paper. JC had thought long and hard about finding Mae and what part of life she would be in, but not knowing would be worst. He had just put his coffee cup to his mouth when Butch started up, "Ok, I did some research last night, and I think we should go to the police station first and see where they think we should start. What's her last name?"

"It's Price," JC replied.

"You can look up just about anyone on the internet," Rebecca replied.

Butch pointed at Rebecca. "Becky is right, let me get my laptop, and we can get on the line."

"Get online," Troy corrected him.

"Yes, on the line." Butch looked at him like he'd lost his mind.

Troy shook his head. "It's called online. Not on the line."

With a puzzled look, "Yes?" He turned to JC rolling his eyes. "I'll be right back."

Gary walked out of the kitchen. "Hang on, Butch. If anyone in town knows anything about this place, it would be the folks at Meat and Three Cafe. I would check with them first; there might be a wait at the police department."

"He's right," Butch replied. "I'll grab the phone book to get the address."

JC interrupted him, "It's just down the road. I know the place."

With that, they headed to the front door and jogged to Butch's 1982 LTD Crown Vic. JC felt terrible about leaving Rebecca behind because he knew she wanted to go, but he wasn't going to get in between whatever was going on with her and Troy.

JC laughed at Butch's car; it was the perfect detective car for the 1980s and perfect for the two old men. It was dark blue with small parts of chrome lining the doors, and each hubcap was painted to match the car.

"Butch, I'd have to say, your car is in mint condition. It doesn't look like you drive it."

"Oh, I wash it regularly. I got me one of those memberships where I can drive into a car wash without paying."

"But you pay for that membership," JC replied.

"Just once. The other times are free," he replied.

JC shook his head with a grin; he was grateful for his new friend. Pulling the car door closed, he glanced at the two-story house to see Rebecca staring out the window. He gave her a small wave, and she waved back like a little kid watching her father leave for work. And for a moment, he flashed back to Mae standing in front of the bus stop waving goodbye to him; it was the last time he had seen her. And the words she spoke to him before leaving had been etched into his mind: life can get pretty fast. I am thankful for our twelve hours together; it has helped me to see that I need to slow down.

With a flash of an eye, they were pulling into the Meat and Three Cafe parking lot. Butch turned to JC. "You ready?" And not waiting on an answer, Butch climbed out of the car and beat JC to the door.

The two men walked into a cafe busy with businessmen, a large table of old men, and a few school-age kids in uniforms. Before the hostess could approach them,

"Anyone been here longer than sixty years?" Butch yelled out with his thick Texan accent.

"That's a pretty long time to be sitting in a cafe, don't you think?" One of the older men laughed.

Butch pointed to the man. "That's our guy." He pulled JC along with him and walked up to the table. "You guys remember a girl named Mae that worked at Gary's B&B about sixty years ago?"

"Son, I'm good to remember my wife's name." The table busted out into laughter.

JC began to become embarrassed with Butch's bold questions until the oldest man spoke. "I remember Mae, cute little thing. She worked at the boarding house because she was pregnant. Can't recall where she was from, though. Seem's like Jefferson or someplace like that."

"Well, that's a start." He looked at JC.

"Actually, she had written that she would stay in town. Hoping to find out what happened to her," JC answered.

"I just remember that she would come in between breakfast and lunch and order a slice of strawberry pie," the man replied.

"Well, thank you for your time. If you think of anything, give us a call." Butch handed him a business card.

The men walked out of the cafe, and Butch paused in front of his car. "I think we should go to the police station." JC shook his head, agreeing, but as soon as they buckled their seat belts, Butch's cell phone rang.

# Chapter 5

"That was Becky! She said she found an article on the line about Mae and the zoo here in town. She also wants us to come get her."

"What about Troy?"

"I don't know. I guess we'll find out. Let's go get her."

With a trail of dust in the air, the LTD flew back to the B&B like it was floating on water. The tires squealed as Butch slid into the drive of the B&B. Rebecca ran down the sloping yard and climbed in the backseat with a hand full of papers. "I printed out the article." She pushed it over the seat and into the lap of JC. "And the directions." She held up a single page. Butch slammed the car in reverse, and with everyone pinned to the back of their seats, he jetted down a side street.

"First, is Troy ok with you coming with us?" JC asked.

"No, but he'll get over it. It's not every day you get to help someone find their first love. I have the address here. Take the next right!"

Butch slid around the corner and blew through a stop sign. JC was about to say something when the three heard the siren from the motorcycle police officer hot on their tail. "I got this," Butch said confidently, rolling down his window.

"License and registration," the officer said.

"Officer, there is a good reason I blew that stop sign back yonder. You see, this is my friend JC. And well, he's dying." There was a pause in the car, and JC's heart rate sped up until he could hear blood pumping through his ears. "His last wish is to find his first love, and that's what we are doing. Can you give us this one pass?"

The office looked at JC and handed Butch his license and registration. "Very well. Just slow down." He returned to his motorcycle.

"Well, that's not reassuring about how I look. Do I look like I'm dying?" JC asked.

"We're all dying," Butch replied. But before JC could answer, they were off again.

They pulled into the zoo, and to their surprise, they were the only car in the parking lot. Together they looked at the gate and the sign that read, Closed Today. JC took a deep breath, thinking about returning the next day when Butch opened his door and climbed out. "Where are you going?" Rebecca asked.

Confused, he answered the question, "To the zoo." He marched on with JC and Rebecca trying to catch up. "See, the gate's open," he replied, then opened the latch.

"No, the gate is not locked, but it is closed; we can come back tomorrow," JC replied.

"Why? We're here." Butch walked in with the two following close behind, looking for employees. Looking around the area, Butch pointed to a building with a sign posted on the side that read Zoo Office. Butch tried the door but found it locked; he looked at Rebecca. "Becky, keep a sharp eye out for anyone." Then he flicked open his pocketknife and started working on the lock.

"Oh, good lord!" JC exclaimed. "What are you doing?"

The door popped open. "Let's check their employee records," he replied like this was something normal for him.

"Do you think they are going to have records from sixty years ago?" Rebecca asked.

"I don't know. But we are fixin' to find out. So, keep an eye out." He entered the office and found a set of filing cabinets. After a few minutes, he returned to the door, where JC and Rebecca nervously waited. "Found them."

"Are you serious?" JC asked and turned his attention to the file that read Mae Price. But to their disappointment, the file was missing any information that would help them find her.

"Can I help you?" A large security guard walked up. JC felt his heart racing again.

"Well, good morning to you!" Butch answered with certainty in his voice. "We are supposed to be meeting Doug here this morning."

"Doug is out of town. Who are you?" The guard narrowed his eyes and pointed to all three of them.

"I'm Butch Jones, the superintendent for the zoo's in this region. This is my team, JC and Becky. We were supposed to meet Doug here to review the employee records and find out who's stealing from the zoo. He didn't tell you?"

The security guard's eyes widen, along with JC's and Rebecca's. "No, he didn't. So, what can I do to help? And stealing? He didn't tell me anything about it."

"You must be a suspect then," Butch said confidently.

The guard pointed to himself. "Me?" His voice squeaked.

"I'm just kidding. Doug said you could be trusted. But what about him?" Butch pointed to an elderly black man carrying a bucket and broom.

"Johnny? He's been here for nearly sixty years. He hasn't stolen anything."

Butch smiled. "Sixty years?" He looked at JC and Rebecca. "You two question Johnny and I'll wrap things up here."

Rebecca took a deep breath, and she and JC approached Johnny. "Excuse me. Can we ask you a question?"

The man stopped and pleasantly smiled. "Yes."

"Did you know a Mae Price that worked here years ago?"

The man thought, looking up and pushing his faded ball cap back with his thumb. "I remember Mae. A bright girl that was always full of joy. She sure was nice to work with."

"Do you know where she is?" JC asked excitedly.

"No." He paused. "She left here and went to work for the library. I never did see her again. I'm sorry."

"You have been more help than you know," Rebecca answered and grabbed JC by the arm, pulling him back to Butch. "We should probably come back when Doug is here." She winked at Butch.

"Sounds good." Butch pulled the office door closed and looked at the guard. "I'll call Doug and make sure he is going to be here next time. You are doing a great job; I'll let everyone know at the head office."

"Thank you," the guard answered excitedly.

The three of them hustled back to Butch's car. "Who is Doug?" JC asked.

"I don't know; I just saw a nameplate on the desk in the office. Figured it was someone."

"If we can get through today without going to jail, it will be a miracle," JC said.

"You're taking all the fun out of it." Butch smiled. "Where are we going, Becky?"

"To the library!"

The LTD peeled out on the blacktop of the parking lot and sped toward the road, following Becky's directions. Briefly glancing both ways, Butch cut the steering wheel to the left, spraying loose gravel behind the car, creating a cloud of dust. As he looked in his rearview mirror, he could see the lights from the motorcycle cop breaking through the cloud. "Well, hell!"

# Chapter 6

"What is the hurry? Is he dying in the next hour or so?" the same policeman asked, pointing to JC.

JC rolled his eyes. "With this driving, I probably won't last half an hour."

The office removed his sunglasses. "Last warning."

"Yes sir, thank you," Butch answered.

The officer returned to his motorcycle while the three sleuths took another deep breath. This day was not turning out the way JC thought, and he had begun to pray that he would make it through until supper.

Rebecca cleared her throat. "I don't know about you guys, but I am starving."

"Me too," JC answered. "What would you like?" he asked Rebecca.

With a childish grin, "Fried pickles?"

Butch waved down the policeman before he could get around them. "Anywhere around here have fried pickles?"

"There is a place called Dill's about three miles down the highway."

"You want to join us?"

"Sounds good, but I better pass. I gotta keep crazy drivers like you off the streets." He sped away.

Moments later, the three of them were sitting around a picnic table outside Dill's, waiting for their order of burgers, fries, and fried pickles. Rebecca had ordered a large cherry soda and was quietly working on it while talking to Troy—who was still mad and still back at the B&B—on Butch's cell phone.

The sky was clear with summer in full swing, the temperature pushing a hundred degrees. After her call, she listened to the men talk about things in the past she had no clue about. "Why did Mae decide to keep her baby?" she asked.

JC looked at her. "I am not sure. Our conversation throughout that night was mostly about chasing our dreams in life. She wanted to help others. I am not sure in what way."

Rebecca went back to her quiet thoughts. She had worked on a mission trip with her church, which had significantly impacted her life. Helping others fit her demeanor; it was the main factor in coming on this crazy search.

Finally, their food came out, and they sat silently while scarfing down burgers and fries.

"You ready to see if Mae is at the library?" Butch asked.

"I know I am." Rebecca jumped up with a half-eaten bag of fried pickles and her cherry cola. "Troy is bored and thinks he wants to join us. Can we swing by the B&B and get him?"

JC smiled at her. "You bet."

After picking up Troy, they pulled in front of the downtown library. Butch searched for a parking spot and decided to stop in the alley beside the building. "Can a car get around us?" he asked.

"I believe so." JC looked out his window.

"You are going to get towed," Troy pipped up from the backseat.

"Nah, I'll pay a homeless person to watch it for me."

"What are they going to watch? If someone wants to tow it, they can't stop them," Troy answered, confused.

"I'll take care of this. You guys go in; I'll catch up to you." Butch walked off toward a group of homeless on the street.

The library was massive for a medium size town; the halls echoed with each step. Rebecca grabbed Troy's hand and smiled that he was along for the search. He just shook his head; it was better than sitting around the B&B all day.

Taking over the search, Rebecca walked to the counter. "Excuse me. We are looking for someone who worked here sixty years ago," she told the man behind a desk.

"I have only been here four years," the man replied. JC sighed at the comment. "But Mrs. Davis has been here probably longer than that. She is up on the fourth floor helping someone with a research paper."

"Thanks." Rebecca bolted to the elevator with JC and Troy behind her.

Butch rounded the corner. "All good; I gave some guy twenty bucks to watch the car."

"What are you going to . . ." Troy started, but Rebecca stopped him, explaining that Mrs. Davis might know.

The elevator doors opened to a creepy fourth floor; it was more silent than the first floor and much darker. They exited the elevator slowly like the Scooby Doo Gang on a mystery. "You guys ever seen Ghostbusters? This reminds me of the ghost in the library," Butch whispered.

Just then, a pale, thin figure stepped in front of them. "Can I help you?"

Butch let out a high-pitched scream. "Ghost!"

After everyone jumped out of their skin, they laughed at Butch. "I'm not that old," the lady replied.

"Are you Mrs. Davis?" JC asked.

"I am."

"We are looking for Mae Price. I believed she worked here years ago."

"I remember Mae. Always reading mystery books. She worked here for a few years, maybe seven or eight. Sweet girl."

"Would you know where she is now?" Rebecca asked.

"No, I'm sorry. I haven't seen her since she left."

JC looked at Rebecca with a defeated look. "We're not giving up." She smiled back.

The lady continued, "She left here and went to work for the orphanage south of town."

Butch put his hand on JC's shoulder. "Was she married when she worked here?" he asked the lady.

"No, she never did marry. Not while she was here. Just took care of that little boy of hers."

"Thank you, ma'am. You have been a big help." Rebecca gently shook her hand.

JC's hopes were higher than ever with his heart rate still up from Butch's scream. The thoughts of Mae working at an orphanage went along with her nature of wanting to help others. A twelve-hour conversation over sixty years ago with a total stranger, and he was about to meet her again. They exited the library into the sunlight that pushed its way through the buildings downtown. Excitement was high, the search was coming near, and JC was going to see his first love. The only thing that stood in the way was . . . no car!

"Where the hell is my car?"

"Where are the homeless people that were supposed to watch it?" Troy asked sarcastically.

Butch looked at JC. "You don't think the homeless man stole it?"

"Did you give him the keys?" Rebecca asked.

"No." He held them up.

Then they heard the rumble of a motorcycle in the distance roaring downing Mainstreet. It was the officer who had pulled them over earlier. He stopped beside them on the street. "When I heard the call that they were towing a 1980s LTD, I knew it had to be you. Why didn't you park in a spot?"

"I figured it was out of the way."

"You guys know this officer?" Troy whispered in Rebecca's ear.

"Yes, long story."

"I got you a cab on the way that will take you to the inbound lot. Any luck?" the officer asked about their search.

"We are heading to the orphanage where she worked," JC answered.

With a salute, "Good luck; I got to go on this call." He pointed at his radio and then sped off, leaving them standing in the smoke from his motorcycle.

"You guys ever broke out a vehicle from an inbound lot?" Butch looked at the group.

# Chapter 7

The taxi rolled up moments later, and Butch opened the back door for the three to climb in, then he took the front seat. After explaining, in much detail, that their car was towed, the driver made a U-turn in the street and headed to the inbound lot. The windows were down enough to allow a cool breeze to fill the cab, and after a short drive, they arrived.

Standing outside the gates, "Here's what we are going to do. Becky, you and Troy go into the office and ask if they have your car here. Makeup something so they have to look on their computer. Then JC and I will go in and see where my car is parked," Butch explained.

"Wait, wait, wait. Are you serious? We can go to jail for this. Rebecca and I are out." Troy backed up, waving his hands.

JC was trying to comprehend the plan and wondering why they didn't just pay the fine when Butch explained, "I have had my car towed a few times and each time broke it out. So, the fine to get it out this time is probably more than the car itself. It'll be a cold day in hell before I pay these con artists."

"These con-artists will put you in jail," Troy argued.

"They are third party, not the government. Ninety percent of the vehicles they tow are in question where they were parked. There was no sign in the alley that said I couldn't park there. It's just one big scam, and I will not give them money for my car."

JC remained quiet, having heard of stories in the past about how inbound lots made money off people who had parked their vehicles in innocent places. He glanced in the lot at the number of cars and trucks, then looked at Rebecca. "You guys don't have to do anything that will cause you problems. Butch and I can do this."

"I didn't come this far with you guys. Let's get the car," Rebecca replied. Troy started to say something but was cut off when Rebecca grabbed his arm and pulled him toward the office.

Butch and JC entered the gates, scanning the parking lot for his car. JC noticed a few cameras scattered throughout the facility. Tapping Butch on the shoulder, he pointed out the three cameras he could see; Butch just waved off his warning before spotting his car in the distance.

"There she is. And nothing is parked in front of her. This is going to be like taking candy from a baby."

JC tried to keep up with Butch hustling to his car while looking for Troy and Rebecca in the office window. Just as they reached the car, JC heard Butch snort. "You ok?" he asked.

Not looking back, "Yeah, why?"

"Sounded like you were having a hard time breathing."

"Breathing? I'm fine."

JC heard the snort again, but this time felt a nudge on his leg. Slowing, looking back, he realized where the snorting was coming from. Standing behind him, with teeth showing, was a short-haired dog salivating at their presents. "Butch?"

"I got my keys. Anyone looking?" Butch said, unaware of their visitor.

JC replied in a nervous shaking voice, "Yes!"

Butch turned to see the dog standing behind them. "Damn."

"What are we going to do?" JC asked, not moving a muscle.

"I got something." Butch quickly unlocked his car and dug in the backseat for a moment before presenting a can of Vienna Sausage. "Poor guy. He looks like he's starving." He bent down, opening the can. "Come here, little boy."

"Little boy? He's half my size." JC's voice shook.

The dog closed his mouth and tilted his head at the can in Butch's hand. He slowly approached Butch and gently took a sausage from his hand. Swallowing it whole, he looked back at Butch. "I got plenty where that came from." He fed him the rest of the can.

"We better go," JC said.

"Agreed. Get in." He motioned toward the backdoor.

"You want me to ride in the back?"

"No, I want him to ride in the back." He pointed toward the dog.

"You can't steal their dog!"

"I doubt it's their dog. Look how poor he is. And if he is their dog, they are not taking care of him." The dog didn't wait for another invitation; he jumped in the back seat. "You staying?" Butch smiled at JC.

JC jogged to the passenger door and climbed in, looking at their new friend panting with his tongue hanging over the seat. Butch fired up the car and peeled out, leaving the parking spot. If anyone had been outside, they would have seen a trail of dust leaving the gate. Butch spotted Rebecca and Troy standing on the sidewalk just down from the lot. Butch slid to a stop just long enough for the two to dive into the backseat.

"Good Lord!" Troy screamed, coming face to face with the dog. The teeth and the growl came back.

"Don't scream; just give him another can of sausages." Butch pointed to a cardboard box on the backseat floor.

With eyes twice their size, Troy looked at Rebecca, who quickly dove and pulled out another can. The teeth disappeared and the growling turned into a whimper. "Poor guy, you must be starving." She switched places with Troy and fed their new accomplice.

"You stole their dog. We can't be part of this," Troy snapped at Butch.

The car slowed down for the next turn. "It'll be all right. We'll find a new home for him."

"We are so going to jail. Stealing a car, dog napping; Lord knows what else you guys did before picking me up!"

"Relax. They'll never find the body. Right, Becky?" Butch replied, looking at them in the rearview mirror.

Troy snapped his head toward Rebecca. "What?"

"It's ok. He's just teasing you." She patted his leg.

"Or is he?" JC replied in a low tone from the front seat.

Troy slid back in his seat, shaking his head, not wanting to know anything else.

"Becky! Look in that box and you'll find a phone book. See if the orphanage has an address," Butch said. Becky pulled out the book and looked up the address.

# Chapter 8

The orphanage was set off the road within an old pecan orchard, the long driveway lined with azaleas and dogwood trees. A few kids were scattered throughout the green fields playing as they pulled up. Butch rolled down the back window and the dog stuck his head out, breathing in the fresh air. His ear's popped up when he saw a couple of boys throwing a football near the parking lot. Once parked, the dog bolted out the window and toward the boys, tongue flapping in the wind. Before the group could react, the dog started playing with the boys.

"I believe the old dog has found some friends," Butch replied, watching the boys running with the dog.

Rebecca and Troy stepped out of the backseat scanning the area at what seemed to be a happy place. "I can see why Mae would want to work here," she replied.

Butch led the group to the office and held the door for everyone to enter. "Can I help you folks?" a lady sitting behind the counter asked.

"I hope so," JC started. "We are looking for Mae Price and were told she worked here once."

The lady looked confused. "What do you want with her?"

"She is an old friend," JC replied.

A man walked out of the office tucked in the back corner. "Good afternoon; I overheard you ask about Mae Price."

Before JC could answer, one of the maintenance men of the property walked in. "There is a big dog playing with the boys out here. I am not sure how friendly he is."

The man walked to the window and pulled the shades apart. "I would say he's pretty friendly; they're playing fetch with him." Then, he turned to JC. "You're an old friend?"

"Well, kinda. I met Mae years ago at the boarding house on Fairview Street."

"And you are?" he asked.

"I'm sorry, my name is JC Davis. These are my friends, Butch, Rebecca, and Troy. They were helping me track down Mae." JC noticed the man's expression turn to concern. "Long story short, I haven't seen her in over sixty years. Is she here?"

The man rubbed his chin for a moment. "I'll be back in a few minutes," he replied to the lady behind the counter. "Come with me," he said to the group.

Rebecca took JC by the hand, and they looked at each other for a brief second. It had been so long since he saw Mae, and after he had decided to find her, he had been practicing what to say. He wasn't sure if it was the soft touch of Rebecca's hand or all the nerves bottled up, but he had forgotten everything he was going to say.

They left the office and headed to another building adjacent to the row of cottages where the dog was playing. Butch laughed at the boys throwing a stick; he figured this was the first time the dog had ever been played with.  The man held the door open for the group to enter a library. "This is a new building that was built for the orphanage three years ago."

"It's nice. Mae works here in the library? Make's sense seein' that she came from the big library downtown," Butch said, pushing his way past the man.

A bronze statue stood in the center of the foyer of an elderly lady reading to two children. JC stepped closer to the statue and noticed the plague beside the figure. It read: The Imagination of a child is greater than the dreams of an adult; hold onto your childhood - Mae Price.

"Wow. She has a statue," JC commented.

"That was donated to the library… in her memory," the man replied.

JC felt a pain like a knife penetrating through his heart. His throat swelled, blocking the news he was trying to swallow. Rebecca grabbed his hand and wrapped her other arm around his pulling him close. JC wasn't sure what to say. The group stood in place feeling defeated.

"So, you are JC Davis. The man who spent twelve hours with my mother before you went off to bootcamp?" If there was any chance of JC speaking, it was gone now. He just nodded. "My name is Joseph Carter Price. It's nice to finally meet the man I was named after." He shook JC's other hand.

With tears in his eyes, JC whispered, "She told you about me?"

"Because of you and those famous twelve hours, she kept me. Of course, she told me about you. Her deepest regret was not pursuing you."

"So, she worked in the library here?" Butch asked.

Laughing, "More than that; she was the director of the children's home for nearly fifty years. Because of my mom, hundreds of children were given a second chance and a good life. As a result, our kids here are highly educated, and many have become leaders in their fields, communities, and homes. Not to mention our military." He turned to JC. "I would love to get to know you. Do you live here in town?"

"No, I live in St. Louis. I am staying at the B&B on Fairview."

"Oh, wow. What better place to hear your story than where you shared it with my mother."

JC felt his arm getting wet with the tears steadily flowing from Rebecca's eyes. "You ok, kiddo?"

"No," she sobbed out.

"Can I give you guys a tour of the facilities?"

JC looked at Butch. "Do you have time?"

"Are you kidding me? You bet we have time. We didn't come this far in one day to just go back to Gary's B&B." He looked at Joseph. "You guys need a good dog?"

Joseph held the door open for the group to exit. "I take it that is your dog?" He pointed to the boys.

"Kinda," Butch answered, seeing the motorcycle policeman pulling into the parking lot.

# Chapter 9

"I knew it, I knew it!" Troy exclaimed. The group watched the police officer park his bike, remove his helmet, and start walking in their direction.

"Well?" the officer asked Butch.

"Well?" Butch replied, confused.

"Is she here? Did you guys find his first love?" He smiled and then looked at the dog playing with the boys. "Wait a minute. Is that the dog from the inbound lot?"

"I believe he followed us here," Butch replied innocently.

The officer looked at him. "Ten miles?" He looked back at the boys laughing and being chased by the dog. He held up his hand to stop any answers or excuses Butch came up with. "Don't tell me." He paused. "He looks much happier here. Plus, I always thought the lot was starving him."

Butch, Troy, and Rebecca walked with the officer to pet the dog while JC stayed behind with Joseph. "Sounds like you guys dog-napped the dog."

"Yes, we did. Not sure what to do with him." JC replied.

"A misfit like him belongs here. We'll let the kids take care of him. What would you think if I joined you for breakfast tomorrow at the B&B? Or is that too much at once?"

"Not at all. I would like that. And I would like to hear your story too."

After they toured the facilities and said their goodbyes to the officer—who never did say anything about breaking out Butch's car—they headed back to the B&B.

Butch and JC talked all the way back, with Rebecca and Troy quiet as church mice in the back seat. Once parked, JC gave Rebecca a huge hug. "Thank you. I would have never met Joseph if it wasn't for you and Butch." She smiled and hugged him back. A hug that felt like no hug she'd had before; in her thoughts, she considered him her grandfather, a person she never knew.

Gary had supper on the table when the four of them entered, and to Butch's delight, his standard frosted mug of local beer was sitting at his place. The four of them enjoyed their last meal together. The following day Butch was heading out to make a few calls and then return home to his wife. Troy and Rebecca were able to change their appointment from that afternoon to the following morning, then they would head back to Arkansas.

Dessert came out and was the hit of the meal, a locally made strawberry pie. Noticing Rebecca had barely touched her slice JC asked, "Are you ok? Do you not like strawberries?"

"No, they are my favorite. I'm just not hungry," she replied.

"You need to eat because the doctor doesn't want you eating after midnight," Troy spoke quietly.

"What doctor?" Butch asked. "Becky, is something going on? Are you ok?"

Rebecca exploded into tears and ran to the front door. Troy started to follow her, but she ordered him back to his seat. She gently closed the door and disappeared to the porch swing. The three of them just looked at each other before JC asked, "You still want to keep this doctor appointment to yourself?"

"It's not my place to tell. You should ask Rebecca."

JC sat his fork down on the table and headed to the front porch. "Can I sit beside you?" he asked Rebecca, pointing to a chair beside the swing. She scooted over to allow him to sit beside her on the swing. She wrapped her arms around him as soon as he sat and bawled her eyes out.

JC rubbed her back as she started to talk. "I came here to have an abortion." She took a deep breath. "Troy and I had only been dating seven months before I got pregnant, and with our lives ahead of us, I didn't want to take away his dreams of college."

"Hey," JC pulled her face up to look her in the eyes, "it's going to be ok."

She swallowed the lump in her throat. "After spending today with you searching for Mae and meeting her son who she almost gave up to adoption, and seeing all those children playing and happy, I can't go through with it."

JC smiled at her statement. "I know we have only known each other for twenty-four hours, but I know that you are going to make a great mother."

"I'm scared. I don't know if Troy is going to stick around. I don't have much of a family and I don't know anything about raising a baby. I just don't know."

"I don't know of any mothers who started out knowing much of anything. I bet all future moms are just as scared."

"I want a baby girl." She began crying again.

"Either a girl or a boy, the baby will be just as pretty as you are."

She stopped and looked up at him. "You are the nicest man I have ever met. I don't deserve people to be nice to me."

"Yes, you do. And I know St. Louis isn't close for you but you'll always have a place if you need it." He helped her up from the swing. "Let's go tell them the news, good or bad, and have a big slice of strawberry pie."

Sniffling, she replied. "I want two pieces."

JC laughed and led her back inside.